THIS & THAT

MEM FOX + JUDY HORACEK

Scholastic Press • New York

For Judy, who does this and that — MF
For Alex — JH

Library of Congress Cataloging-in-Publication Number: 2016016825

ISBN 978-1-338-03780-7

10 9 8 7 6 5 4 3 2 1   17 18 19 20 21

Printed in Malaysia   108
First edition, February 2017

I'll tell you a story of this,
and I'll tell you a story of that.

I'll tell you a story
of cavernous caves
and a chimp
with a magic hat.

And then . . .

I'll tell you a story of this,
and I'll tell you a story of that.

I'll tell you a story
of two little boys,
who raced down
the road with a cat.

And then . . .

I'll tell you a
story of this,

and I'll tell you a story of that.

I'll tell you a story
of crazy giraffes,
who tried to sit on a mat.

And then . . .

I'll tell you a
story of this,

and I'll tell you a story of that.

I'll tell you a story of kings and queens,
who loved to have a chat.

And then . . .

I'll tell you
a story of this,
and I'll tell you
a story of that.

I'll tell you a story of two speckled hens,
who were terribly, terribly fat.

But now . . .
it's bedtime.

So . . .

I'll tell you a story of that,
and I'll tell you a story of this.

And I'll tell you a story
of how I adore you,

And then . . .

I'll give you
a KISS!